HANDS

HANDS

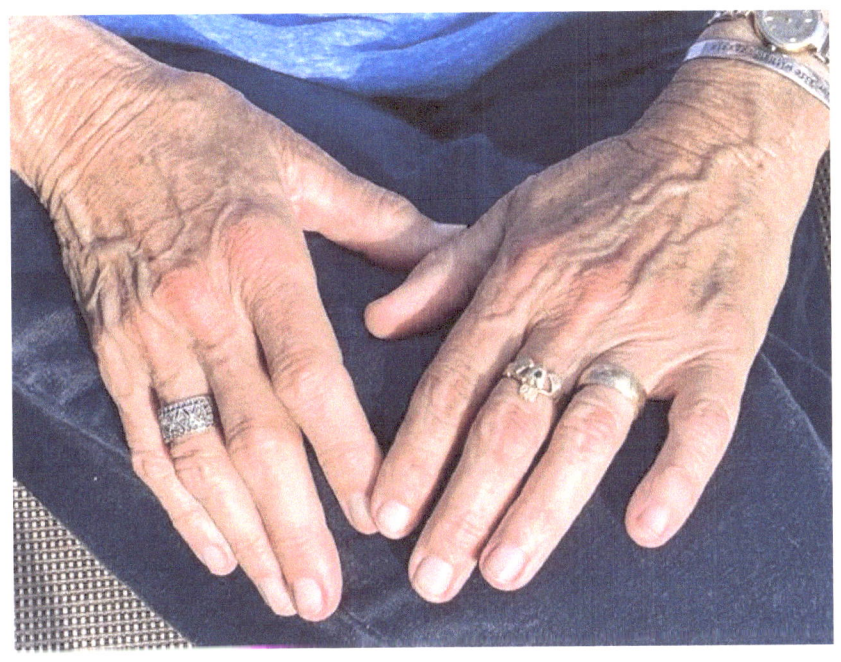

Poetry by

Thomas F. Wylie

PEAR
TREE
PUBLISHING

HANDS

By Thomas F. Wylie
Copyright © 2025 by Thomas F. Wylie

Published by Pear Tree Publishing
Bradford, Massachusetts
www.PearTreePublishing.net

Proudly published in the United States of America

Wylie, Thomas F.
   Hands / by Thomas F. Wylie

   ISBN 978-1-62502-062-8
   Library of Congress Control Number: 2024913969

   1. Wylie, Thomas F. 2. Wylie, Thomas F. – Poetry. 3. Massachusetts – Untied States – Poetry 4 Poetry - Modern I. Title II. Wylie, Thomas F. – Poetry

Cover & Book Design by Thomas F. Wylie
Photos by Thomas F. Wylie

1 2 3 4 5 6 7 8 9

Introduction

The poems in this volume are about the pain and joy of life, especially while growing up. Self-awareness of one's life never comes easy; seeking to evolve, understand, accept, and grow as a human being. I was fortunate to have encountered teachers, friends, co-workers, writers, and thinkers who influenced my sense of self and the world. Chief among these in my early writing efforts were some masters, Goethe, Rilke, and Walt Whitman. And more recent poets, Robert Bly, Donald Hall, and Sharon Olds.

Also, I was assisted by contemporary poet Susan Donnelly and her excellent writing classes and readings with fellow students in the Boston area. Alfred Nicol of Newburyport Powow River Poets was instrumental in providing key writer insights such as, *all adjectives are suspect,* and *only emotion endures*. And Dan Speers of Haverhill, MA, of Native American descent, with a remarkable poetic memory and ability to recall and recite the works of many poets. His collegial work with the Haverhill River Bards has been invaluable.

This volume is arranged in three sections: Part I The Early Years, Part II Coming-of-Age, and Part III Reflections. Each concludes with a poem about hands.

"I think of you daily, but it isn't even you"
"The Father" - Sharon Olds (1992)

Table of Contents

Early Years

Part I

I was born in Albany, New York on March 29, 1944, when WW II was raging in Europe and the Pacific. At five we moved to a rented house on a steep hill overlooking a creek in a tiny village called Brookview, New York. The location is about 1.5 miles from the Hudson River and two miles from Castleton-on-Hudson, a town of 1,500. At that time Brookview had a general-store post-office and one-pump gas station, and a two-room schoolhouse for grades first to third in one, and fourth to sixth in the other. Learning to read and understand did not come easily nor did an awareness of my parents' great divide and dislike of each other, which remains a life-long memory.

Grey Fedora

Polished wool, back rim turned up, front
tipped forward, grease stains along the
outer edge from the rub of your fingers.

Perfect crown indented down the middle
insides lined in white silk and leather
band stamped with CFW, size 6 & 5/8.

Your dress-up hat kept in the rear seat
window; worn Sundays never on the job.
On a rainy Halloween night, I stole it,

pulled it over my ears crushing its crease.
It tainted me with the smell of your sweat,
Brylcreem, and rage. Years after you died

I found it in a storage box, still with a faint
scent of you. I took it for the last time.

Red Flowers

Mother's Day again, and you are long dead
I remember red flowers for a special grave.

You, choosing this day each year thinking of
her, a grandmother I never knew, with whom you

shared a one-room home in servant's quarters,
struggling until she became sick and died.

The flowers were always red, I never knew
why. I stood back and stared at the cold stone,

watching you plant them, reliving thoughts of her.
Feelings unknown, kept from me yet passed on,

memory of your memories.

Time Piece

Lord Elgin Shock Master,
14 karat gold, inscription
on back:

> *Safety Award to*
> *Cyril F. Wylie, 1958*
> *Five Years No Accident*
> *John Vogel, Inc.*

I was 14, you'd been gone
two years. I knew nothing, only
you left and drove trucks.

The watch appeared amongst old
socks and underwear after you
died March 29, 1979, at 2:05AM,
on my 35th birthday.

What did this watch mean to you?
Pride, happiness, disgust? Did you
want me to find it?

The watch speaks to me, of time
together, we never had.

Inside its mechanism are secrets,
secrets about

> where you were
> who you were with
> why you left, and

didn't have time for me.

Captive

Youngest of four sisters eager to marry
Everyone warned her, to be wary of him.

Homelife was a prison without iron bars.
Caged, she was a bat in a tunnel of shouts.

First binges and welts then teeth knocked out.
Ashamed, she discovered how to hide bruises.

At night, after years of being divorced and
alone, she stares out windows, sleepless and

locked-up.

Name Taken

Ashes on a shelf boxed away
a handful scattered glitter-like
into a creek.

A memory in each passing
speck crystallized into stone.
The last of three generations

that bumped and ground
into and away from others
decade after decade. Genes

transferred one to another with
uncertainty, making someone
out of so very little.

That sucked and grew to bump
again, into others; with care and
nurturing nipple to headstone.

Eternal passage of words and silences
enveloped with echoes of the dead
homage to your mysterious gifts

felt in a purr-greeting of our cat,
sips from fresh coffee, discarded
notes and buttons, an emotional

dust bin of wanting to forget
in nightmares coughed-up
sweated-out gagged-on.

Perhaps this bead of sweat from
eyebrow to chin is your gift that
accompanies me this day.

If We Could Relive Again

Time recalls nothing but what is spent
Time only knows that which we say is so

If We Could Relive Again, there be no relent

When we cried together under your bed
Time froze us as we listened in fear

If We Could Relive Again, the bad we'd shed

Time brings joys and sorrows from the past
As children we had no idea of what lies ahead

If We Could Relive Again, I'd remove our mask

Suppose time was an all-forgiving cure
Our pains and sadness would not be so

If We Could Relive Again, we'd be secure

This and That

When we were growing up
it was not happy nor carefree.
Life was secrets, and worry, what
could happen to you and me?

Bruises, fights, shouts, fear.
We hid under my bed staring
at Mom and Dad's closed door
the fighting loud and near.

My first awareness, surprise
at the sound of a hard slap.
You whispered to me, they're
doing more of this and that.

We noticed neighbors and friends
for whom food and money was
not in short supply and laughed,
wanting to stop our cries.

Different from others we knew,
Dad drove nights, slept days
we crept around the house to
not awaken his angry ways.

He earned the money, had
the car and held Mom back.
All we could do is watch and
hope for an end to this and that.

Cold Car

dark gray 1958 Oldsmobile
four-door dual exhaust
soft cloth seats
new car smell

red lipstick-stained butts
under the front seat
with newspaper rolled
half-pint, exposed

driver's window open
taste of cigarette smoke
with rush of cold air onto
a backseat face of frozen

disgrace, sunken and
staring with mirrored
eyes of hate

Gift I

The day was a nothing
dark, rain, cold, wind and
misery; end of March.

Fourteenth birthday
no big deal
a nothing year.

Saturday and home alone
not even a ring from our
5-way party line phone.

The dog needs to go
chasing me room-to-room
begging to piss.

I open the door to let him out
and then see what I missed

A shiny new blue bike
leaning against the wall
in the entryway hall

I stare from the threshold
as the dog races out
Is this for me?

I touch and smell the dark leather
seat, kneel and hug whitewall
tires and chrome rims. And

wonder: how could I pout and cry when
something special was just outside.

Gift II

Alone with you in the hospital room sharing
our silent awareness, the end is near. It's March
again, worse weather of the year.

Your words are few, only grimaces of pain
you motion to me mouthing my name
I lean close, my ears to your lips.

"Get me out, take me home!"

What to do, a last request? With uncertainty
I shout for the nurse and tell her

I'm taking him home, now!

On a gurney in the ambulance, your
last ride alive is rough and bumpy
I drive behind slowly taking in

our common reality with flashbacks
from years of anger and strife.

The new bike appears from twenty
years back. With tears I see and feel
our father-son confusion and attacks.

Our shared last journey with this,
my feeble attempt at giving back.

Scar

pajamas crumpled on the floor
blood lines blot green cotton
sticky and sore to the touch
patterned red-dark on purpled skin

was leather made for this?
buckled with brass
to beat an ass?

snow freely drifts
inching up the inside sill
wet and compactable
slamming at heat from the radiator
cauldron of cold and hot
screaming at hearts
that never thaw

silent solo moans
rock back and forth
stab at the ugly

"That did not happen!"

prayers for spring
held and blocked
by hate seeds buried
in February tundra

swift strike and shout
mirror image and sound
eternal throughout

Late for Dinner

I kept calling Tommy, but he didn't respond I knew he was in the school yard as I could see the front wheel of his bike in the faint light, and as I looked again, I saw him jump on the bike to ride the short distance toward me and when he arrived he spoke excitedly about the one-handed-left-field catch he just made as together we lifted the still-shiny-new blue bike up and into the entry way and laughing went into the kitchen for dinner I prepared for the four of us with

his sister and father sitting with their food at the table waiting for our arrival and his father acting very impatient while giving me a hard angry look as we took our seats and Tommy said, *Oh mom, not meat loaf again I hate meat loaf* with the last word coming as the huge callused right hand of his father reached out wide and struck a swift surprise slam to the left side of his head as he with chair and glasses flew hard onto the floor and me screaming, *Stop it, you are hurting him,* as his father stood, flinging his uneaten plate of food at the kitchen sink then stomping out loudly with banging thumps from his black engineer-booted feet with a shout

Serves him right, stupid dumb-ass kid.

The Empty Seat

Red Star Express notice to all drivers
NO passengers allowed in company trucks

There is grease on the back of your knuckles
the color of the huge steering wheel

deep black like the spots
on back of your right hand
that held decades of Lucky Strikes

Did you get permission to take me
because it was only a hook-up
cab to tandem trailers?

Your stained fingers are the color of muted yellow
like the yellow spade in the shed at home

Your face pitted and pock-marked from acne
as if carved from a moonscape.

My friends fear your face,
tease me

Why is your dad's face like an ugly Man in the Moon?

I stutter

He had a hard life

and let out a fart that
sent us to giggles

And now I sit in your discarded car
and observe your empty seat

I smell your presence
feel your absence
and see

your hands on the steering wheel

Let Go

> *"...let go your hand from my shoulders,*
> *Put me down, and depart on your way."*
> "Leaves of Grass" - Walt Whitman (1855)

Let go your hand from me

> Keep yourself away
> Keep yourself astray
> Keep yourself in decay

Let go your hand from me

> Stay away let me be
> Stay away do not see
> Stay gone from inside of me

Let go your hand from me

> Never a pleasure to me
> Always with hate of thee

Let go your hand from me

Fall

I thought it was someone else, no
the body is mine, flat on my back
looking up after slipping off the roof.

I heard faint voices and shouts
"God dam, his arms are bent back,"
inside I knew nothing, but doubts.

I tried to rise and was feeling sad.
when I heard my friend Lee say, *"No,*
don't move, you're hurt really bad."

It seemed forever until adults arrived,
my father in wrinkled baggy workpants,
who silently stared as if I was dead.

And even longer till the ambulance
came. Volunteers constantly saying,
"Stay awake, tell us your name"

I was fourteen; six decades hence I
stare in the mirror. What if this event
that froze my father in time

had never been mine?

Attempt

playing baseball
late coming home till nearly dark

front door wide open a hot August night
house lights all on

shiny-new green car Friday-night-regular
in the driveway

in the kitchen
my sister is sobbing
I go toward the sound

fire and smoke
in the kitchen sink
I rush and douse the flames

money is on fire
wad of twenty-dollar bills smell is like burnt paint

a door slams
the green car roars guest man is going

my sister still sobs
on the basement threshold
cellar light is on and

I see a noose made from
extension cord that
connects the steam iron

to the kitchen wall socket
black long thick
with a special plug-in

it hangs high
hooked to a back step
over the cellar floor

Kitchen Stare

*"It is easy to love people in memory; the hard
thing is to love them when they are in front of you"*
"My Father's Tears and Other Stories" - John Updike (2009)

You remain on the fridge door, faded and dusty
      I've looked at you endlessly, wedged
      between our daughter and two sons

Though you have been long dead your stare remains
      a laser beam aimed at me with a warning,

      "You better be good"

Shrunken in stature having lost inches in your last
      years; abundant hair still yours, neatly
      in place, and bed-sheet white

I knew what you were thinking, read your lips as
      I snapped this shot.

      *"Tom, I'd like my dinner now,
      and please refill my wine"*

This was our mother-son pattern, the push and pull
      tell-me-what-to-do forever relationship that
      I loved, and despised

While not visible to others, I see your scars and
      know of the pain and horror they hide,
      the tears, screams, and lies

Of the four of you that day, you'd be pleased to know
      three are well; sons grown, daughter now a
      mother of our two grandsons

You remain the only absent one in this photo, a
      silence that continues to speak

Generations of Darkness

sex grabbed
stolen and released
jabbed with force and fullness
blind to shouts cries screams

blood semen sweat
mix with joy and dread
spilled to earth
hardened to skin

merge and succeed
to make an unknown
to you and to me

some grow and suck
many more do not
cast into graves and
fields of grass
water and fire

dry bones brittle teeth
soil to seed
connected to
the grip of need

dark to light
and dark again
endless millennium
tiny traces
twist turn
and bend

Vacant Lot

Another drive-by, they seem endless
unavoidable in our one-horse town

how many car-passing window views?
more than I want to remember

I think it was 1982, the house fell
backwards down into the creek

my bedroom in the back, second
floor over the unheated garage

in its falling parts must have hit
the rocks and rapids below

We first lay together in that room on
my bed madly kissing and feeling

lucky for us, my mother banged on
the door,

"Knock knock, that's enough!"

just as my hand touched your breast,
the first anyone had ever done

As I look now there is nothing; just dead
weeds, black-top, a tire, nameless junk

dumped scattered tossed, where our
two-story rented house once stood

a dreary ghostly lot like my memory
of us, fallen and discarded

Father

The memories return each day and night
although you have been gone these many
years despite your absence, I feel a cold fright
powerless to the pull of boyhood tears

I watched your angry arm throw a plate
from a blanket spread beneath a shaded tree
aimed at a woman there who was your mate,
which decades later, seems targeted at me

Ignorant man never learnt a better way
distance and coldness continued to grow
as my confusion became ability to say,
what your wake distorted I did not sow

Over the years in which we did not speak
remains the comfort, we shall never meet

Absence

Before

I was ten when I realized September 1st
is your birthday

we never observed it nor spoke of you,
you were never there

And your age? We didn't know
mother did, but it was

forbidden to speak of you
except for shouts and swears

when the food money did not arrive

During

It was 3:30AM on my 35th birthday
March 29, 1979. I was dreaming you'd died

when the call woke me with the news.

Dreams can be real.

How to react when your father dies,
and his only presence was

a lasting sense of anger and hate?

I went through the motions; even
touched your cold rock-hard hands

before you were lowered into the ground,
with me staring; what could this mean?

After

You've been dead nearly 40 years,
your absence still present

the pain has lessened but returns
in full each September 1st

when I write you a letter, my life
long effort to understand

what might have been

the sense of loss has not diminished,
a softening awareness has emerged

you did the best you could, I suppose

I struggle to ponder what a real
father-son life could have been

yet realize you never knew your own
father, he died when you were two

your pain passed to me

Hands 1

His hands are mottled and speckled with colors
like sunrise on a cloudy sunny day, with blue,
pink, grey, and orange. And brown, deep dark
dime-size spots of ugly brown.

These are hands of death, that will feel and touch
for only a short time. I hold his left; warm and dry,
limp with lifelessness.

These hands lived a life of trucks, beer, body odor,
cigarettes, quick sex, ugly apartments, anger, hatred.
A wake of shame and ill-will clings to anyone
who depends upon these hands.

His hands held reins, gripped steering wheels, connected
cabs to trailers, pumped gas, and delivered hundreds of
gallons of beer and whisky to his lips.

The right hand held the power of a swift mean prize fighter,
a huge hairy hand of scars, dirty nails and thick calluses
which could whack with the force of a knockout punch.

The right was for the hand slam, which would come so
quickly I did not feel the pain, my dinner of peas, meatloaf,
and mashed potatoes sent airborne with me,
hard to the floor.

At the end his hands are crossed on his lap in his box,
cold and stone hard.
I reach in and shiver, touching them for the last time.

Coming of Age

Part II

Brookview is a rural area of dairy and vegetable farms and orchards and a small number of commuters, such as my father, who worked in Albany ten miles north. A high school drop-out at sixteen, he drove horse-drawn wagons, then taxis, and finally a teamster job driving long-haul eighteen-wheelers. He worked nights and slept days while my sister and I went to school and our mother worked as a part-time bookkeeper. Family life was a struggle, money always short of what was needed, lots of cigarette smoke and drinking, and many arguments. At eighteen, I graduated high school and left home the next day. Brookview years never let go.

Rearview
for HG

It began with a locker slam
in the hallway before first period.

She giggled as I dropped papers
and lunch bag on the floor.

"Sorry, you're funny and I'm
late for French!"

Wow, what happened? Does she
like me? No, couldn't be

Then it was the soccer game
against Avril Park High. Me as
defender, scored a wrong goal.

At the half I slunk back to the
bench hearing boos and jeers.
Coming up behind me she said,

It's fine, go back and get'em!

My heart leaped with joy.

Then a first kiss in my car in
her driveway as the porch light
blinked on-and-off, signal to
stop and get inside.

I drove home in a daze singing.

Dates, ice skating, walks, prom,
graduation and summer jobs.

Off to college; she to one, me
another, 100 miles apart

a string of efforts to hold on,
go steady. It ended. She found
another. I'm still looking back.

Schoolhouse

When we met, I was a lonely boy entering
First Grade with Mrs. Douglas.
You were the big white giant in our tiny hamlet.

Holding two classrooms, large open closets to take off boots,
store lunches, hang coats and rain gear,
and a common hallway entrance with restrooms
and a long rope to the brass bell above.

Each room had four to five rows of
wooden desks facing the chalkboard.
I was in the second seat row one
near the windows facing the ball field.
The row was First Graders, second and third rows
Second Graders, and fourth row for Third.

The second classroom held grades Four, Five and Six.
They were the big kids you avoided if possible.
My sister Pat was in Fourth.

Outside, your shiny clapboards were huge and wide,
with tall windows.
There was a dirt path all around you for races and games.
One side no windows, we played wall-ball against it.

General Assembly each morning;
attendance taken on your concrete steps,
all pupils lined-up soldier-like as the flag was raised,
and we recited the Pledge of Allegiance.
Mrs. Douglas read the day's Announcements,
and we filed in row by row to assigned rooms and seats

You protected us in those first free uncertain years
of our lives. Taught us to "duck and cover,"
allowed us to share stories, and sheltered us
in rain, sleet, and snow. Lunch hour was special.
We opened boxes and bags of treats,
ate quietly and listened as Mrs. Douglas read
the next chapter of "The Box Car Children."

A to Z at Brookview Elementary

My first-grade desk was row one, seat two, behind
Harvey, the tallest and dumbest in school,
Who no one liked to play with.

Harvey was closest to Mrs. Douglas who said,
our morning lesson was learning letters A to Z

I was told to get the boxes of letters from the closet
and to *"Do a good job of handing out the letters"*

Boxes were green cardboard, old and torn from use

I gave a box, each with scrambled letters in color,
size and shape, to every first grader. We were told to
correctly make the alphabet on our desk for inspection.

As I sat down, I heard a box fall to the floor and letters
scatter around Harvey's desk, spilling into row two, which
made second graders laugh, one said *"He's so stupid."*

Harvey was crying and Mrs. Douglas went to him
and said, *"Try and do your best and be neat."*

She turned to me; I smelled perfume and her breasts came
close to my face as she whispered:

*"Help Harvey pick-up and put them in order. Tomorrow he'll
go to a school for children who need special help."*

I got on my knees next to Harvey to help, his smell was awful.

I did a bad job of handing out the letters.

Oh, how I love thee!

As the snow falls
and the ladder shakes
you call to me while
passing the snow rake

Did you know your socks stink?
And I must remind you, your
dishes were left in the sink

As I scrape and pull from the top rung
at the four-foot drifts of snow and ice
I am thinking if this ladder slips

Despite our years of love,
this won't turn out nice

Oh, how I do love thee
in this time of snow-emergency

How you hold firm the ladder
to prevent my fall, yet still
continue your chatter

How we are so alike and different too,
and now a stormy Valentine's Day from
which we will look back and say,

It's always been something new

Peaks

My peak is in the AM
your peak is in the PM

Isn't it amazing somehow,
we remain close friends

My color is green
your color is yellow

How amazing together,
we're so mellow

Your social pace is fast
while my pace is slow

It's amazing, somehow
our love still grows

You Went Downstairs

to begin making our morning coffee
emptying old grinds into the trash

adding fresh cold water to the pot with
four scoops of Verona dark roast from

a newly opened bag of Starbucks when
I join you and turn on hot water to

warm our ceramic cups and set them
on the counter to be ready for pouring

just-brewed coffee which we both know
is essential for the start of our day

I was Preparing for Bed

and started to disrobe when you
came onto the bed with eagerness

brushing my arm with affection
as I sat to remove my shoes

you came to lie along the length
of my right thigh as I reached down

to untie my laces when you rolled
slowly part-way onto your side and back

I reached to stroke you, as you looked at
me with longing, and purred wildly

Wood Pile

Am I ready?
Weeks of lifting, hauling, and stacking? Late August, seize the moment or price goes up. I agree to delivery and call my son Tristan; get the tarp, splitter, ax, work gloves and water, and move a half-cord from last season. Tristan arrives looking slow and tired, I'm reminded he has a hernia. We open the tarp, out slithers a green-eyed snake, he jumps back and shouts, "What the fuck"! I bark; "It's fine, he's looking for a place to winter, help out!" The truck arrives and drops two cords of oak, maple, and hickory; light in color but good length for the stove. The sun beats us as we slowly sort and stack one of nine rows. My back aching, I take two more Aleve. Tristan's wiped out, can't or won't move another piece while I, the old-man keeps at it hearing my wife shout "Don't go crazy; don't kill yourself!" October arrives, the temperature drops to the low 40's; we fire up the cleaned stove.
At long last the payoff begins.

Water

The cold wrinkles skin from toes to nose
when up for air from dive below; gasping
air, goose bumps and chattering teeth

Water, great escape from the dreaded place

From Moordener Kill, "Murderer Creek"
to the mighty Hudson of wide shores and
inlets perfect for setting muskrat traps

Water, doesn't know or say my name

offers dreams of life beyond; being gone
cast off, stowed away, float away, stay away

Water, innocent channel of the possible

constant flow of joy and wonder on its
shallow surface or deep down under

Water

Love Mix

Sunday afternoon
60-degree January day
the house was empty of children.

We lie down after a morning of
diapers, breakfast, trash, laundry
we clutch and embrace with
desire for love and connection
yet only energy to sleep.

We awaken hot and longing
pulling at each other's clothes
driven by separate need.
We entwine kiss and stroke
sex follows; slow, and playful.

"No more babies this better not connect"

I moan half in agreement yet pleased
with the possibility.

We hold a long embrace thinking of
our ties to one another, moments of joy
and sweetness that come too seldom.

Weeks speed by, your cycle stops.

You book a termination appointment
and we avoid each other.

I seek refuge in the basement with the leaky pipe.

When the date comes you call for me.

"I can't do this!"

We hug in a moment of recognition.

I return to the basement and
weep with joy.

jabs and stabs

hot hot heat – inside the insides – and outside too
all on top, where oh where is that ugly spot?

synapses synapse
fire spitting thoughts and wear
cognitions of fret everywhere met

a foot slips a stick snaps

God dam it, I lost it!

I stumble and fall – scratch and haul
is there a seer inside with smarts?
a trickster grabbing a frozen heart

suddenly it appears, your gray and ugly
headstone, rigid and cold like what lies below

Just smash the sucker – beat the hell out of it!

reach in reach out – loot your mind
the damage is done
there is no time

Stay dead on your floor lie in wait for your whore

images out images in who's to say

what is a sin?

Edge

Feels so close
easy to peer over
to see the longest
way down
no one around
no-way to be found

crisp cold blade
dark and sharp
gleaming and eager
to make its mark

breath to breath
stealth to stealth

thin strong long
dig deep
go for gone
prune clip cut
narrow the hedge

where's the edge?

Accident

His bedroom is quiet and still,
undisturbed by years of absence
My mind cuts to the past; stuffed

animals, braided rug with vomit
spots, middle school novels, baseball
cards, photos, and repaired teddy bear

Observing, recall of that awful night
traumatic head injury, unconscious,
ambulance, fight for life

When I arrive at ER it's a sea of tubes,
cries, and medical workers. I remain
for a long sleepless night in a waiting

room of fright, with one small light
awakened by nurse every two hours

"No change, still stable"

I lay cramped and sleepless on
a green polyester nothing chair

At last, a nurse shakes me awake

"He's coming about"

I stagger and stumble to the ICU
bright lights, medical staff. Nurses
and doctors pause and step back

Tristan opens his eyes, flails his arms and
reaches for me

"Dad, Dad, get me out"

We cry and hug across tubes and people
exhausted, he falls into his deep dark night

Shift

Week's end at last
daytime work time
so full so fast

Monday to Friday
grab and pull at time
take-me-here take-me-there
do this do that push aside
what's mine

Seasonal shift heat lifts
cold descends
time drifts light shifts
when and how shall we
make amends?

September, Virgo transitional point
joys of warmth and sun
dissipate with thoughts
and preparation of
cold to come

January, first of year
recently so very near
and now with
the end in sight
how is it the feeling
is so like the
coming of night?

The cycle continues
the turning is here
arms of time and change
going on and on
an endless game

holds us all
summer to fall

Sleep

I never know what comes with sleep
whom or what I may chance to meet.
No matter the time of day or night,
a person or event to fear or greet.

Sometimes I wake filled with fright
someone stabbed me with a knife!
I sweat, toss, turn, and try to flee,
then wake up, shaken by my wife.

She shouts *it's a dream can't you see.*
I stare and mumble, what happened to me,
and realize I've had a bad night.
I prop myself up, seek to be free.

I ask why sleep brings me a fight
When I seek a peaceful rest at night
Sleep with rest seldom comes out right
Sleep with rest seldom comes out right

Summer to Fall

Pale green yellow orange and brown
season's new colors visible all around

happens no matter who sees feels or not
in awe I sense the presence of nature's plot

time and change has shifted since that day
tears dreams memories regrets all stay

in your apartment I scan items that remain
knowing without you life is never the same

how to live with loss that won't go away
eats at me no matter work food dress or play

I speak gently as I can seeking to hold back the pain
fearful careful as to when or if I say your name

Calling

Aloneness, friend, or foe
who's to know?

with me always

Wrinkles in my trousers
lost buttons and pins
hand-gestured *"hello"* to strangers,
rabbits dart across my running route

inside my head
distant voice

Running a meeting, facilitating words
she taps my shoulder,
pulling back
50 seconds 50 miles 50 years

Hands to face eyes closed
gasping for air
she pulls and pulls
directing to

squeeze this pen
spill this ink
quickly, quickly
before I emotionally,

                        sink

takes my breath
sucks my breast
gives constant pause

will she ever part?

Father, stone-cold in his casket
mother, morsels scattered
across the creek; behind where
home used to

                        be

Sealed ashes sit quietly on a shelf
invite dreams that should have ended
with the last

                        breath

Once we were four
Now we are two
But who knew

Were there more?

How can we be so close
And yet so far away at
The same moment?

A crow calls from outside
awakens thoughts from the
locked-body-skin of existence

offers energy
that wants to
rush out the window

dear crow

                        let me fly with you

Close Call

fall, fall, falling
leaves, limbs, branches
      emotions

free falling
missed center line
car drifts to the edge
on its own power

Friday afternoon
highway to home
a near miss

falling and drifting
on the road into
unknowns light to dark
missing
      the in-betweens

dreaming – wedding ring falling
from my finger – downhill
down and down
spinning away
vanishing at its own pace

like a relationship, a marriage
bond of love and friendship
altering weaving disappearing
moment by moment via
        collected absences
        words not spoken
        gestures not shared
        calls not made

waking up one day from
a dream to ponder,
        is this
        what there is
        to this?

did we fall that far?
has the emotional center
        lost its way?

Last Commute

Awake and roll right
clock blinks 4:25 AM
Monday morning week begins
stomach churns time to rise

Visions of driving highway ahead
100 miles of white-knuckle grip
freeway anything-can-happen-way
Haverhill, MA to Warwick, RI

I get up and see Ki-Ki the cat
who spits up in my path,
I jump to avoid the mess

Turn on the light, pick out suit,
shirt, tie; clean up mess, head
downstairs to kitchen

Turn on coffee, feed the cat
bring in paper, check the
weather report, roads OK?

Gulp two cups of French Roast, take
two Advil, shower, shave, dress, eat
and pack the car.

5:50 cheek-to-cheek kiss with wife
and into the car; rain, sun, snow or
ice, I must go!

How many years of commuting?
How many round-trip miles? Endless
      10 years of 200 miles a week to Rhode Island
      5 years of 100 miles a week to Maine
      13 years of 60 miles a week to Boston

28 years of commuting; 7 cars
12 sets of new tires
hundreds of fill-ups
scores of oil changes
batteries, engine issues
two AAA roadside assists

A life of gripping the wheel
as the body and mind are
whizzed at highway speed

Now, at 70 years of age
the last commute for the
last day of work

The moment is unreal
all I can see is endless
highway, traffic, dodging in
and out; eyes ahead and back

Hoping beyond hope I can
make one more round-trip

You're too good to be true*

From the bus window I see your smile and waving
arms as we pull into the Amherst town common

    I can't take my eyes off of you

Warm cheeks press and hold me tight in the fall air

Years of struggle, change and pain, diapers,
clothes, jobs, cars, and rent

who could know what living together meant?

    You're just too good to be true

Target for a thrown can of tuna at my head when
harsh words passed the point of acceptability

A missed projectile that scored a memory and
added a dent to our intersected lives

Sweaty gasps gave way for older bodies that ache and
like chipped clapboards need constant re-touching

Yet able still, to share a side-by-side thrill

Fearful of greater age ahead yet accepting the past
as anchor for the unexpected, you remain

    too good to be true

*Frankie Valli, (1967)

Hands 2

Her hands are those of experience; they lift
her three-year old daughter and while she holds
her, hugs and kisses me longingly the daughter
turns away unable to feel what she sees.

Her hands caress me, hold me, stroke me, bring me
spasms of immense joy and pleasure day and night
month after month. Hands of passion and moisture,
which seek what they desire.

Her hands hold and rub her expanded womb,
and guide mine under hers. I feel the quick
movements of life inside. I am awed with joy,
surprise, and tears.

Her hands go to her face which is contorted
with pain and anguish. *"It's time"* she shouts,
quickly I move to action mode of rehearsed steps.
Phone calls, car keys, blankets, and directions.

My hands are first to hold him; he is a crying sack
of pleasure in my arms which shake and tremble.
Gently I hold him, carry him, and place him for the
first time in her hands.

Her two hands with my two, four hands together,
raise three pairs of hands with years of diapers,
meals, books, bills, joys, sorrows, and tomorrows.

We sit holding hands, hers are knotted, fingers twisted,
knuckles swollen. Lupus courses her bones, life is difficult,
movement uncertain. A lifetime with hands that now
endure pain day and night.

Reflections

Part III

As the realities of adulthood deepened I met and married a life companion who has been a major part of my efforts at seeing the totality of who I have become. The transition of writing daily journals, fifty years of them, eased as I explored the shorter and more powerful discipline of poetry. This last section offers reflections on facing the draft, racism, personal struggles, and observation on maternal hands that were dear to me.

Immigrants

skin, blood, breath, eyes, teeth, and hair
I'm connected to each of you by dreams,
hopes, fears, land, sea, and air

chains made; chains broken; they do
nothing but hold, torture, kill, push,
pull, imprison, or release the unspoken

parched earth, green grass, birds in flight,
clothes to carry, babies to hold, for thousands
of years, millions, and millions, by day and night

why, where, how; borders, fences, barriers,
mountains, rivers, snow, sun, sleet; what
ever obstacle we struggle on our feet

accepted, rejected, jailed, or set aside, how
is it that so many make it and thrive yet turn
cold backs toward thousands that die

you, me, we, they; all of us "others," on lands
that were not of our fathers and mothers

Scare Tactic

It began with a short hang-up call and a scream,
"You dirty commie"

So, I just left the phone off the hook

It was mid-November 1972; McGovern had just lost the
election, meaning four more years of Nixon
and the Vietnam war

We knew the war must be stopped

We planned a major public demonstration for noon at the
Post Office, many vowing to block access, chain ourselves to
the doors

I was a principal organizer with the mimeograph machine in
my bedroom, and holder of the bank account for our anti-war
funds

Notices went out with my name and address seeking support

Along with cash and checks… hate mail arrived.
The worse threatening to get me and
"Cut your balls off"

Demonstration day was cold but sunny;
we decided not to block the Post Office

Angry war supporters appeared but were outnumbered,
the police keeping us apart and peaceful

I returned to my car to see a note taped to the driver's
window

"God hates you; you'll go to hell"

Not Me
to Bob Dylan

December 31st, 1969, Selective Service lottery,
number 324, arrived and I knew
I would not be drafted before I turned 26 in March.

I erupted in relief and verse to Dylan's *It Ain't Me Babe*,
shouting to the Uncle Sam "Babe," burning my draft card,

"I'm not the one you need"

I'll not go to Vietnam; not kill

*"to protect you and defend you whether you are right or
wrong"*

This was no easy choice, close to signing up with the Marines,
deciding to complete college and serve in the Peace Corps,

1967 to '69, teaching in the Philippines,
and then a year in VISTA,
as the war... raged on and on; thousands killed and injured.

The number 324 meant an end to eight years of anxiety over
the draft and Vietnam. For Uncle Sam, I would not be

"...someone who will die for you and more."

In the US and the world hundreds of thousands protested
the war their voices telling me.

"And anyway, I'm not alone."

Shoe Talk

Where have you been, not worn me in months
abandoned after 300 miles

I'm sorting through running shoes for wear and
wondering; keepers, giveaways, or trash?

When I pick up a pair of faded New Balance 990's,
high end $160-dollar shoe, with tongue open and,

I see what you did. Moved on to Brooks and now
Hoka; the fancy Bondi 6 with red laces

This closet is dark and crowded, full of your favorites,
they all stink!

Thinking I must be dreaming I grab the 990's
give them a quick look, and select for trash

Ouch! Don't you get it? I'm better than that; for
odd jobs, cutting the grass, and when it's icy I can
keep you from falling on your ass!

OK, I think; perhaps there is more life to these
but my wife will say, out with them, please!

I continue to toss out old boots, dead slippers,
and flip flops with broken tongs

One last look at the old 990's and into the
barrel. Am I crazy or did the shoes just say

don't do this!

Keepsake

Did you throw out my running shirts?
can't find them anywhere, always kept
them at the bottom of the closet near my
shoes, boots, slippers, and stuff

Yuk, some of those go back to the '70's
yes, I tossed out a few, time to throw out
old clothes, can't find a thing in that closet

What! Why'd you do that, one of those is
my first marathon shirt, 1977, running with the
Sugarloaf Running Club in Western Mass, I ran
my PB, Personal Best of 3:02

Well damn, let go of some of that will ya? If you
want them they're in trash bins in the garage.

Pivoting quickly, I dash to the garage and to the
giant barrels each overflowing with kitchen trash,
dirty kitty litter bags, and a dozen or more bright
red Target plastic bags knotted at the top

I rummage and dig; finally, at the smelly bottom I
see one plastic Market Basket bag and recognize
several of my old running shirts

I rip open the bag and there it is at the top, bright orange
Sugarloaf team singlet with my white blue-lettered 1977
Ocean State Marathon shirt.

Sunday Morning Run on a Fall Day

Lacing up running shoes to go
on seeded lawn that's failed to grow.
As neighbors peek out at the day
he pauses, stretches, and starts slowly.

The sky and clouds are a mix of gray
he wrestles with a problem, what to say?
Not able to see the splendor abound
wanting success, come what may.

Reaching mile three he turns around
and looks up from darkened ground.
The brilliant colors shock him still,
offer a calm he's seldom found.

At mile four he speeds up a big hill
the early hour leaving time to kill,
and a problem resolved to his will.
A problem resolved to his will.

there is no time to grieve

no time to grieve
for your absence
when you're always present

the fifteen steps leading to your room
bathroom sink with abandoned toothbrush

no time to grieve
when I prepare your favorite meal of stewed
tomatoes, cheese with meat balls

no time to grieve
when I park my car in your
favorite parking spot

no time to grieve
when I dropped your special cup
and it shatters in the kitchen sink

you standing nearby watching

grief is the price I pay for loving you when

there is no time

Stand-in for Godot

I waited and waited
oh, God, how I waited.

Raggedy, standing in the cold
pacing back and forth.

A one-act, me, and myself
Vladimir and Estragon,

two-person performance,
musical without music.

Talking full speed; is he here?
no, he's there, but soon he'll be

here while still there, and then
I can be here and there.

Now he's coming but wait,
who's that, Pozzo & Lucky?

This is so like me, wanting to
be two people so now it's four.

Self within self in twos and so,
its double the trouble; and

only one certainty, there
will not be a curtain call.

White

The benefits of skin color appear
at the oddest moments, like

when last in a checkout line of fifteen,
all black but me, and a white drugstore
clerk looks directly at me and speaks

"May I help you?"

Or when you're seeking a city apartment
the owner offers if you help him find
other tenants you get a month rent-free,

looks you straight in the eye and whispers

"But remember, we don't rent to blacks."

White

unspoken privilege
never comes off

everyone sees it

Ode

"I had never honored you as a living equal"
"Ode to Dirt" - Sharon Olds, 2016

Dear Sharon, I too take dirt for granted
upon which I spit, piss, dig, and dump trash
without thinking or feeling. Not that I
don't know it's there; its everywhere.
And filled with the dead. Billions of bones,
body parts and pieces; animal, plant and
Homo Sapiens beneath hills, fields, water,
and ice caps. I witness remains scattered,
lowered into dirt; know of millions killed
and mutilated in battles to stake
flags. Earth's peaks and valleys worshipped
and desecrated. What meaning we cannot
fathom. The selfishness we bequeath shall
be our leavings as we reenter dirt's embrace.
Your Ode is prescient, universal worship
and alarm of what's to come. May this
Ode to your Ode be a salute to those who
enrich the earth doubly; spoken sonnets
above, over organic remains below.

Name Taken
to Paul Robeson

Name-in-name-out; decades and decades
of glory, hate, success and blocked out

There's a man going 'round taking names taking names

In with Princeton, Phi Beta Kappa, Cap and Skull,
The Emperor Jones, Body and Soul, and *Ol' Man River*

Out with "*I want to be African*," support of the Soviet
Union, Crusade Against Lynching, and being Communist

he's been taking my father's name and he left my heart in vain

In with "*Joe Hill*," *Ballad for Americans*, and *Othello*.
Out with Trade Unionism, the FBI, and the Peekskill Riots

Paul Robeson: fifty years of known and unknown pain
love and hate without freedom to explain

All American, NFL player, highest academic honors and yet
despised, disgraced, and shadowed by those he never met

There's a man going 'round taking names taking names

Passage of time and genes; arrival of new names,
little of his life known nor proclaimed

Generations roll on; stories appear and reappear in a country
that resists history, and the truth behind a man

who was robbed of his name; and

left my heart in vain

Charleston, SC

November 14, 2015

A conference brings me here
up at 5:30AM dark and cold

prep for an early run with
deep thoughts and purpose

I seek the place of loss, an envelope
inside my orange-glow jacket

On Calhoun Street, I ask a fellow runner,
where is Mother Emanuel Church?

Its number 110, just up the street half-a-mile,
I'm on a long run that way, I'll show you

We jog along, talk of the killings and this city in remorse
yet over-shadowed by today's terrorist attacks in Paris

Permanent scars just five months apart

Suddenly a large white wooden church on the left,

there it is good luck to you

I wave goodbye, and pause at the flowers and memorials

In seeking the mail slot, I touch a huge granite step,
and wonder, a foundation stone from 1816?

The slot is at the bottom of a weathered wooden door,
I insert the envelope with a note and donation

I stand and say a prayer, and bow
A despised flag came down, at what cost?
I look east as the sun rises, and jog on.

Finish your dinner or no dessert

I am! I hate turkey. The beans are ugly!

Meals eaten, prepared, shared and fought
over, for years it was a meal for a deal.

Eat this you get that, it's good for you,
your body needs it, finish, or no TV

I cook this time you cook next
Whose turn tonight?

Yours, you had a meeting the last two nights
I'll feed the cat I want to relax

We evolve from decades of sit-down-to-eat,
and everyone helps; to

Grab-and-go-take-out, you make yours I'll make
mine, left-overs pick-and-don't-complain

How could it be different this time? Turkey or no turkey,
fixings?

And then, I run a road race and win a turkey.

a 13-pounder for a sit-down-all-together dinner

I carry the bird home and make room in the fridge
three days to thaw and plan the meal

Turkey day arrives

We dust chairs and arrange four around the circular
Butcher-block kitchen table

After four-and-a-half hours
the turkey is a perfect deep bronze color.
We add chopped fried potatoes, salad, cranberries,
mac and cheese, fresh hot bread, Pinot Noir,
and desserts of cake, pie and ice cream

A moment of thanks, a rare meal of connecting.

Sitting

Sit here I do and wait
       wait for something
       that may
           alter my fate.

Sit here I do, a waiting room, where
       I've squirmed and sat before,
       dry mouth stomach churning
       what shall I say this time?

Where to begin with a beginning
       shall it continue
       or shall it end
       will defenses go up
       or reason descend?

Yes, oh yes, I've been here
       before, waiting in a room
       outside a closed door.

Who holds my fate, leads
       me to the lock
       that unlocks
       the knot?

Channels and courses
       paths and aisles.
       I wander, skip
       surface, and am placed
           into someone's file.

Bad Writing

bad handwriting sometimes leads to new ideas

First Grade teacher Mrs. Douglas shouts,
"your script looks like chicken scratchings on paper"

After standing in coop shit

Chickens don't care, their strutting continues as
do lines like streaks from a palsied hand

Why write if no one can read your writing?

Chickens eat whatever is on the ground,
I pick and pluck whatever jumps into my head

Scribbled lines live on in this country of barnyard
chickens digging the earth, scratch by scratch

Chickens fear not death,
only the ax makes them quiver and shake

Bad writing

"Bad People"
"Morning Poems" - Robert Bly (1997)

Without you

No matter how long, you remain gone

you appeared in a dream last night,
struggling to surface in deep water

I could not reach you

awoke in a wet sweat

Awaiting the EMT's you whispered to Lin
he's going to be pissed at me

downstairs, I hold door for men and gurney

Days and months pass, time stands still

At a social event with colleagues from 20 years
back, friendly chatter, then one says to me

lost two brothers this past year, hurts everyday

Why does someone else's loss lighten my own?

We did not know in time events overtook reality,
twelve hours of tears and holding your hand, we left

without you

Summer Writing

What to choose what to lose?
A reading; something new, something
old, perhaps long dead or just stuck cold

My summer and writing didn't mix, guilt
and emotions ran wild

Thought about, talked about; present,
lurking in doubt

And the muse? Without a peep,
took the slip

Readings took place; Guest Poet at one,
and one-of-four at "Prime Time Poets"

Words, emotions, and sounds went into
rooms of people

some stayed around

And now at season's end a stir, a twitch,
an itch, has begun

New verbal life peeks from the heat
to push out, and rise from the deep

June to September, lines, and images,
too few to remember

At Mom's

Put your dishes in the sink, rinse them out!
how many times do I have to tell you?

Yup

You never listen to what I say, now look at you;

GET YOUR FEET OFF THE COFFEE TABLE!
When are you going to grow up?

Working on it.

Did you order the part for the garage door?
I'm so tired of having to lift and close it.

Affirmative

And when will it be here?

Not in my control.

Well, what is in your control? You drive me crazy!

Yup

Whoa, where did you get the bags of bagels?
Enough to feed the whole neighborhood.

Store

Well of course I know that, but which; the Deli,
Panera's, the Bakery?

Yup

You're totally impossible;
I ask a simple question and get no real answer.
Where did you learn to talk?
You never used to be like this.

Yup

And stop with your stupid yup, yup, yup!
You sound like an ignoramus;
an idiot who never learned anything
Your father and I did not raise you that way,
and don't talk like that!

Oh, yeah

Eight Ways of Looking at Cancer

1 Define it

skin, lung, kidney, breast, prostate
colon, rectal, bladder, pancreatic
thyroid, lymphoma, uterine, cervical,
undetermined, add yours

2 Ignore it

unpaid parking tickets
dying embers in the fire
spam calls from Nigeria

3 Deny it

get second, then third opinion
complaints of your bad breath
engine warning light

4 Face it

the car is out of gas
you didn't need the hair
we all go sometime

5 Hate it

for the loss of loved ones
for the pain that does not end
why me?

6 Embrace it

pimple scars from adolescence
your parents did their best
friends are always late

7 Fight it

drugs
appointments
make a bucket list
swear at God

8 Accept it

get a wig
last will and testament
millions went before you
update your bucket list

6-6-16

Was it only a dream?
what could it mean?

100 years ago, this day
Born a woman who
became Grandma Kay

She made it to 91 with
thoughts and worries
about her only son

He wrote and wrote,
lines and thoughts
without ever sharing

what he had wrought

Verses now in the family tree
that forever connects her

to his eternal question, what

of the remains of me?

Self Portrait With Memory

Living in the present a challenge when the past
is never dead, refuses to let go

Memories poke haunt and surface like the wide
swinging leather belt that beat ten-year-old flesh
for the crime of making noise

Images tumble out at unexpected moments

Alone with my grandmother holding her moist hand
at the moment of her last breath, a life-long shiver

The dead aren't dead, their voice reappears as
does my mother's jab *"you've given up on him,"*
about a fraught relationship with my son

Twelve years gone, the words sting like yesterday,
ring with doubts of self-worth

Memory doesn't stop; it's paint that never dries

Hands 3

Her hands touched, felt, folded, and scolded
for 95 years. Her hands held books, turned pages,
washed dishes, drove cars, ate chocolates, and
hid pocket change for me to search and find.

Her long lean strong hands grabbed me, held
me, prevented a fall off her fire escape to a sidewalk
twelve floors below. Never again did I sneak out her
living room window in Queens.

As I now hold her hands, they are limp, warm, and
soft. Dry scaly shrunken; wax paper-like, visible blood
lines and transparent skin. Bones stark white

My mind buzzes with thoughts and speed
from a white-knuckle four-hour drive,
western Mass to southern Connecticut.
Desperate impulsive wrenching sweaty anxiety
to be with her.

Her wrinkled hands are cold and stiff as the monitor beeps.
I look up and see a blue line go flat as she leaves me, alone
at her last moment of living flesh.

I loved Grandma Mack; the New York City born
rock solid family matriarch bookstore manager
who raised four daughters alone and hated all men.
Except me who could do no wrong despite the truth.

Her hands were fired to ashes.
Scattered over Long Island Sound, as close to
New York City as possible on a cold September day.
Hands of protection now eternal.

Acknowledgements

The author is a member of the Haverhill River Bards.

He is grateful for inspiration and guidance from:
Arlington poet Susan Donnelly,
Newburyport Powow River Poet, Alfred Nicol,
and Haverhill's Poet Laureate, Dan Speers.

Several poems appeared in an earlier collection by the author.
Cold Car, (2014)

And in the following publications:

Cold Car, *The Lowell Review,* (2023)

Cold Car, Late for Dinner, Attempt, Let Go
http://www.bewilderingstories.com/bios/wylie_bio.html

Scar, Rearview, Time Piece
https://sites.google.com/site/classactpoets

Merrimack Mic Anthology V, (2019), edited by Isabell VanMerlin
Oh, How I Love Thee, Aliens, and White

Merrimack Mic Anthology IV: *Watershed* (2018),
edited by Isabell VanMerlin. Father, Grey Fedora

Word Play a virtual exhibit of poetic art, (2020)
edited by Isabell VanMerlin, Last Pose, Wyeth Selfie

Merrimack Mic Anthology VIII: (2023),
edited by Isabell VanMerlin.
This and That, Self Portrait With Memory

Also, by the author:

Haiku Unmasked, Perspectives from the Pandemic, (2020)
Byron Petrakis, editor,
with Cheryl Lauriente Rossman, Cassandra Petrakis Zwahlen,
and Thomas Wylie

Cold Car, (2014)

About the Author

Thomas Wylie lives in Bradford, Massachusetts near the banks of the Merrimack River. Born in Albany, New York his childhood years were in Brookview, a rural community south of Albany.

After receiving a B.A. in history from the State University of New York at Buffalo (SUNY), he began his career teaching for the Peace Corps in the town of Pototan, on the Island of Panay in the Philippines.

After that he served for one year as a VISTA (Volunteers in Service to America) in Waterloo, Iowa.

He worked for several years as a community organizer prior to graduate studies at the University of Massachusetts, Amherst from which he received an M.A. in Communications and an EdD. in higher education. He has worked at several colleges in Massachusetts, Maine, and Rhode Island.

A life-long runner, he completed fifteen marathons, including five Boston Marathons, and a 50-mile ultra marathon.

His first book of poetry *Cold Car* was published in 2014.

He may be reached at tfwrun@comcast.net

Tristan Harris Wylie

January 15, 1986 – December 7, 2023

Praise for Thomas F. Wylie

HANDS:

The Roman poet Catullus wrote, I hate and I love. Tom Wylie writes as simply, and as powerfully. Take for example his poem, *Let Go*, a poem so in-your-face it's like the barrel of a gun. Its repetend is a line of Walt Whitman's, Let go your hand from me, and it is addressed to his father in his grave. The speaker himself cannot let go of his revulsion. His words are charged with painful emotion from start to finish. A declaration of independence is, of course, a declaration of war.

Many of Wylie's best poems deal with the kind of emotion that usually gets buried and goes unsaid: the self-doubt of an abused child; the loneliness that is part of the human condition—Aloneness... with me always; the heart's panic when a relationship unravels... One poem sets forth a matter-of-fact catalog of the unremitting pain of losing a child: no time to grieve / for your absence / when you are always there.

Others sing of joy and wonder in the presence of new life and innocence, of lifelong gratitude for a grandmother's nurturing kindness, and of love that extends beyond the family, of solidarity with all of us 'others'. The light these poems emit is all the brighter for Wylie's courage in facing the darkness. Those that glow the warmest are the ones that celebrate the happiness, solace and contentment he has found in a loving marriage —including perhaps the only love poem in which the beloved hurls a can of tuna at the poet's head!

Alfred Nicol, *Nationally recognized and award-winning poet*

Thomas Wylie's aptly-named book, like a pair of hands, is a fingerprinted chronicle of a personal history. With heart-wrenching honesty, he takes his father's hands, feels once again their brutality, tries to come to terms with that relationship. He chronicle's his wife's hands through the ups and downs of their life together; his valiant grandmother's are ashes scattered over the Sound "as close to New York City as possible." He grieves the loss of a son. Yet along with unflinching looks into his personal life, Wylie's poems also speak to a passionate involvement with his times: civil rights struggles, antiwar protests, a reflection on "the benefits of skin color." Some lively poems even describe his wide experience as a marathon runner. To read **Hands** is to follow a life, revealed with great honesty and skill.

Susan Donnelly, *author of The Maureen Papers and Other Poems*

Yearning for Connections: *the* **Hands** *in the Mirror*

One advantage a reader of poetry has over the poet is that the reading of poetry is essentially a private affair. One can find poignant lines, meaningful insights, and perhaps even an explanation or intuitive connection to their own feelings or memories insecurities, but in the end, despair or hope need not be revealed in public.

The poet, however, bares all, often revealing his or her innermost secrets, emotions and attempts to uncover the hidden meaning of life, love, and longing. Especially when it comes to family. So it is with **Hands**, a sensitive and expressive collection of poetry by Haverhill poet Thomas Wylie that chronicles his own experiences in growing up and coming to grips with reality in a world trapped between love and hate, nightmares and dreams.

One gets the sense of inner conflict and introspection from the very two poems in this collection, the **Grey Fedora** that introduces the poet's father, and **Red Flowers**, the mother, poems on facing pages that immediately mirrors the internal struggles that gave rise to and illuminates this captivating collection.

What begins subtly transpires in a series of reflective poems, each like first two poems and in many ways the ghosts of father and mother, facing each other with, the author's remembrance that only recalls the trauma and emotions of the past and the future but reflects the introspection of a poet trapped between two mirrors and the reflections of pleasure and pain, past and future, repeating back and forth, over and over again in the mind of the poet in the middle.

The poems, with their vivid imagery, transport us to a different world, one where the beauty of the language is as raw and unapologetic as the emotions it evokes and the sudden shifts in sight and sound and even smells, like in **Cold Car**, the *"new car smell"* sublimated by the *"taste of cigarette smoke"* with the juxtaposition of the haunting lines that in and of themselves mirror the conflict, *"a backseat face of frozen/disgrace, sunken and staring with mirrored/eyes of hate."*
These poems remind one of the greats like Emily Dickinson, William Blake, and Sylvia Plath, whose words continue to resonate ages after they were first written. Their works, like our poet, are a testament to the power of poetry; how it can *mirror* the essence of humanity and lay it bare for all to see as what comes in the poem, **Scar** *"swift strike and shout/mirror image and sound/eternal throughout."*

We are taken on a journey, through the past and into the future, exploring the complexities of love, loss, and longing. Wylie's words, so carefully woven together, speak directly to the heart, mirroring the poets deepest fears and desires. In a world where we often feel disconnected and lost, poetry is a beacon of hope, offering us a sense of belonging and understanding.

At times, the discordance and dislocation are almost palpable, the yearning to find a sense of home in a place one cannot call their own, yet so poignant that anyone who reads these poems cannot stop, cannot wait to see what happens next, what truth is revealed and the mirror cracks, as in **This and That**, "*not knowing what/could happen to you and me?* when all one could do *is watch and/hope for an end to this and that.*"

Wylie's poetry is both a search for connection and a celebration of the fragility of human emotions, reminding us that it is our vulnerability that makes us truly alive and it is his title theme, **Hands**, that reach out both in search of and to grasp both the raw emotions and capturing the essence of what it means to be human. And in our search for connections in a world that is not truly familiar, Wylie's words serve as a guide, a beacon of hope that reminds us that we are not alone in our struggles and our triumphs.

And it is hands that reach out in lines, "*your **hands** on the steering wheel, ...touched your cold rock-hard **hands**, His **hands** are mottled and speckled with colors, These are **hands** of death, that will feel and touch, These **hands** lived a life of trucks, beer, body odor...* One could on. There are so many lines, so many references. "*Her **hands** in my two, four hands together... A lifetime with **hands**... Her **hands** touched, felt, folded, and scolded ...*"

That last reference to hands is from **Hands 3** at the end of the volume. In our hearts, somewhere in the dim recesses of our lost genes and forgotten ancestors, we all have a Grandma Kay. What "*remains of me*" is the memory of what "*Her **hands** touched, felt, folded, and scolded for 95 years.*" Wylie's poem is a reflection of the human experience, delving into the depths of our emotions and mirroring the past and future in our search for connections.

The yearning to find a sense of home in a place you dare not call your own is a sentiment that resonates deeply with readers. Yet, amidst the pain and vulnerability, there is a glimmer of hope and truth in your words. This is what keeps readers coming back, eagerly waiting to see what happens next and what new truths will be revealed.

Hands. Either they show the puppet how to dance or they control the heartstrings. And, ultimately, as the poet Wylie writes in **Hands 3**, even when the hands are "*fired to ashes,*" they are "***Hands** of protection now eternal.*"

Dan Speers, *Poet Laureate, Haverhill, MA*

COLD CAR:

Cold Car is a bold new voice of family, love, and real life. These are poems from the gut and memory that will resonate with anyone who has looked into his/her past and thought deeply about what it all means. Wylie describes events in his family and life that will get you thinking about the meaning of your life and what really matters. Wylie captures those times of our life that stand out. Read this when you have some time to be with yourself.

Michael Jacoby Brown, Author of *Building Powerful Community Organizations*

As Malorie Blackman tells us, "Reading is an exercise in empathy; an exercise in walking in someone else's shoes for a while." Reading Thomas Wylie's book Cold Car takes you on that journey. Filled with all the emotions from living life, Wylie speaks in words we all can understand.

Christopher P. Obert, Founder of the New England Authors Expo